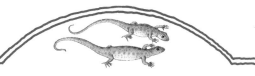

LITTLE LIBRARY

Cinderella

AND OTHER STORIES

Retold by Margaret Carter
Illustrated by Hilda Offen

Kingfisher Books

NEW YORK

KINGFISHER BOOKS
Grisewood & Dempsey Inc.
95 Madison Avenue
New York, New York 10016

First American edition 1994
2 4 6 8 10 9 7 5 3 1
Copyright © Grisewood & Dempsey Ltd. 1993

Library of Congress Cataloging-in-Publication Data
Carter, Margaret.
Cinderella and other stories / retold by Margaret
Carter; illustrated by Hilda Offen,
p.   cm. — (Little library)
Contents: Cinderella — The princess and the pea —
Aladdin and his wonderful lamp.
1. Fairy tales. [1. Fairy tales. 2. Folklore.] I. Offen,
Hilda, ill. II. Title. III. Series: Little library (New York,
N.Y.)
PZ8.C248C1   1993
398.21—dc20
[E]   93–5770   CIP   AC
ISBN 1-85697-968-7

Designed by The Pinpoint Design Company
Printed in Great Britain

Contents

Cinderella

Charles Perrault

Once upon a time there were three sisters—two older ones, not very pretty, not very nice—and the youngest, who was both pretty and nice.

The two older girls were jealous of their pretty young sister, and so they made her do all the work. "Light the fire! Hurry up there!" and so on.

By evening the poor girl was so worn out that she'd just sit by the fire to rest.

"You're always sitting in the cinders," said the sisters. "That's what we'll have to call you—Cinders, Cinderella!"

Now the king and queen of the country were giving a big party for their only son, hoping to find a bride for him. Invitations were sent out, and what excitement there was when one came for the sisters!

"We must have new clothes, new shoes," they cried. "Oh, we shall both look so delightful the prince will surely want to marry one of us."

"May I come to the ball?" asked Cinderella. "No!" said the sisters. And that was that.

On the day of the party the sisters took ages to get ready.

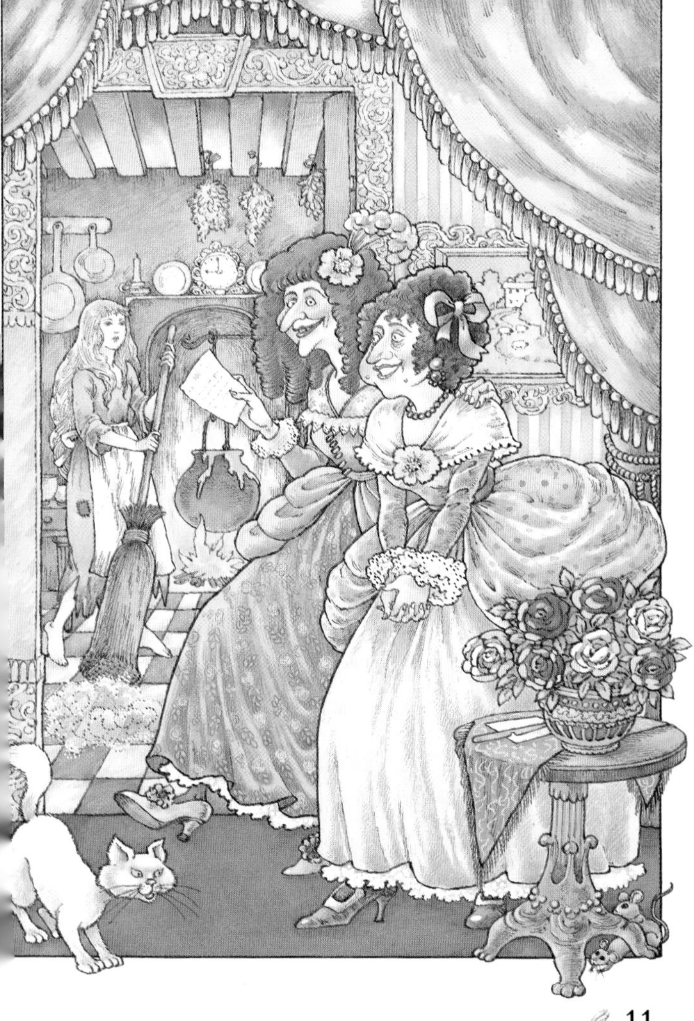

They changed their clothes, lost their shoes, tried on different wigs, gloves—you've never seen such a hullabaloo in your life.

At last they were ready, and off they went, leaving poor Cinderella all by herself.

Sitting alone by the fireside, poor Cinderella felt very sad indeed. One big tear rolled down her cheek and fell into the ashes, plop!

"Don't cry," said a gentle voice, and there was a most beautiful lady.

"I'm your fairy godmother," she said, "and I know you want to go to the ball. And so you shall."

"But I have no coach," said the girl, "no horses, no fine clothes."

The fairy smiled. "Bring me a

pumpkin from the garden," she said.

Cinderella brought the pumpkin. The fairy gave it just one tap of her wand—and there was a coach, golden and shining.

"Now," said the fairy, "bring me the cage of mice you'll find in the kitchen."

She waved her wand again, and instead of six little mice there were six plump horses ready to pull the coach.

In the same way a rat became a fine coachman, and two lizards were changed into footmen.

"You must have a dress," said the fairy, and again she waved her wand—and there stood Cinderella in a most beautiful dress. On her feet were tiny glass slippers.

14

"But remember, Cinderella, the magic stops at midnight. You must leave the ball before the clock strikes."

When Cinderella arrived at the ball everyone wanted to know who this lovely stranger was. The prince danced with her all evening, and the

girl had never been so happy…. And then, suddenly, the clock began to strike twelve! With a cry of alarm Cinderella ran from the palace, but as she did so she dropped one of her slippers.

The prince ran out after her, but she had vanished. He picked up the glass slipper. "I will marry the girl this shoe fits," he declared.

They searched for days. Tall girls, short girls, fair girls, dark girls, all lined up to try on the slipper. But not one did it fit, until they tried the three sisters. For the first it was too

17

narrow, for the second too tight.

"May I try?" asked Cinderella, and it fitted! At that moment the fairy appeared and with one wave of her wand changed the girl's rags into a ball gown. The prince was delighted to find her again, and they were married in no time. So it all ended happily.

The Princess and the Pea

Hans Christian Andersen

There was once a prince who wanted to marry a real princess, but although he searched he couldn't find one he liked. He came home feeling sad.

One night there was a great storm—thunder, rain, lightning—and in the middle of it all there was a knock at the castle door.

"Who can that be?" asked the king.

Outside stood a young girl, soaking wet, sniffling, and shivering.

"What are you doing out on a night like this?" asked the king.

"I'm a princess," said the girl. "But I've lost my way."

"She doesn't look like a real princess," thought the queen. "We'll soon see about that!"

So while the girl was taking a hot bath, the queen piled twenty quilts and twenty mattresses on a bed. But underneath the first one she put a small, hard pea. The bed was now so high that the princess had to climb a ladder to get to the top, and was quite out of breath when she got there.

"Sleep well," said the queen, smiling to herself.

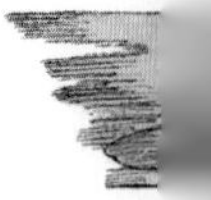

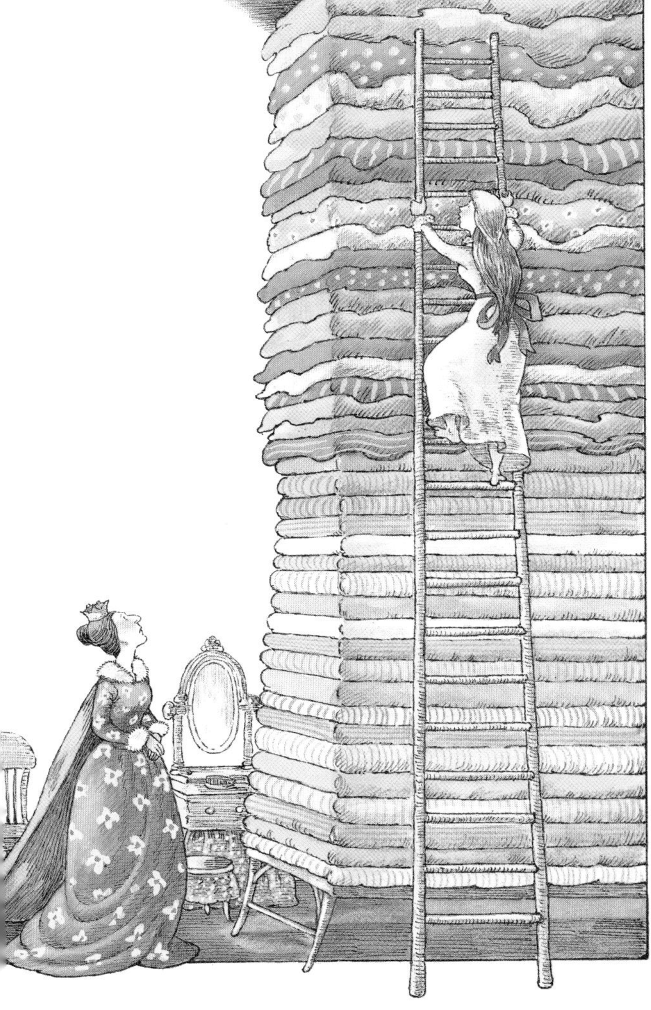

Next morning the princess was the last one to come to breakfast. She looked terrible. "Didn't you sleep well, my dear?" asked the king.

"You're very kind," she yawned, "but there was such a lump in the bed!"

"Aha," said the queen, "only the soft skin of a real princess would have felt that pea through all the quilts and mattresses!"

The prince was delighted to have found a real princess, and after the wedding he put the pea in a glass case in the town museum for all to see.

Aladdin and his Wonderful Lamp

Arabian Nights

Far, far away in the land of China, a boy was playing with his friends. Up and down the streets of the city they ran, too busy to notice that they were being watched by a tall, bearded stranger. At last he spoke to one of them. "Would you help me find something I've lost?" he said. "I'll pay you well for your trouble."

The stranger showed the boy, whose name was Aladdin, a big slab of stone set in the ground. In the middle of the stone was an iron ring.

"Lift the stone," said the stranger, who was really a magician, "and you will find a cave leading to a garden. At the end of the garden is a lamp. Bring the lamp to me and I'll give you many gifts. And here is a ring to show I will keep my promise."

Aladdin put the ring on his finger and climbed into the cave. He soon found the lamp, and on his way back he picked some fruit in the garden.

The magician was waiting for him. "Quick, give me the lamp," he cried. "Help me up first," said Aladdin. "The lamp!" shouted the man, and as they struggled with each other, the stone fell back into place.

Aladdin was trapped in the cave!

The magician, now that his plan had failed, ran away as fast as he could.

"How can I escape?" thought the boy. Still wearing the magician's ring, he wrung his hands in distress. Suddenly, flash! there was an enormous genie, bowing and smiling. "I am the genie of the ring," he said. "What is your command, Master?"

"I'd like to go home, please," said Aladdin very politely.

Next moment he was at home, and his mother was admiring the lamp he'd brought.

"Aladdin," she said, "we could sell this lamp. I'll just rub it a little to make it shine...."

No sooner had she rubbed the lamp than whoosh! there stood another genie!

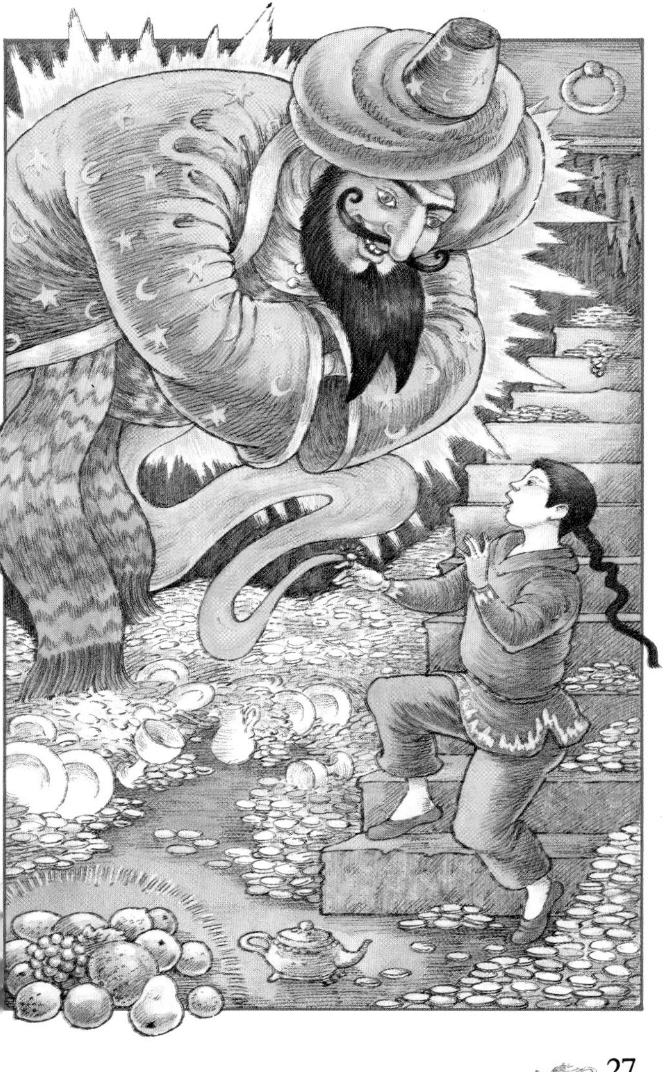

"I am the genie of the lamp," he said. "Your wish is my command!"

"We'd like some food," said Aladdin, "and nice clothes and a better house." And there it all was!

"Anything else?" asked the genie.

"Yes," said Aladdin, "I'd like to marry the Sultan's daughter!"

"Take her the fruit," said the

28

genie—and vanished.

As soon as the Sultan saw the fruit he realized they were precious jewels. "This man would make a good husband," he thought. "Could you build her a palace?" he asked.

"No problem," said Aladdin, and by the next day there it was, with a red carpet for the princess to walk on to her new home—all thanks to the genie of the lamp.

LITTLE LIBRARY

Red Books to collect:

Beauty and the Beast
and Other Stories

▲

Cinderella
and Other Stories

▲

Goldilocks
and Other Stories

▲

Little Red Riding Hood
and Other Stories